This book belongs to:

Emress

Written by Ronne Randall
Illustrated by Estelle Corke

This edition published by Parragon in 2013

Parragon
Chartist House
15-17 Trim Street
Bath BA1 1HA, UK
www.parragon.com

Printed in China

Daddy's Little Girl

PaRragon

Bath · New York · Singapore · Hong Kong · Cologne · Delhi
Melbourne · Amsterdam · Johannesburg · Shenzhen

Emily lived with her mommy, and daddy,
and baby brother. Emily was a very
busy little girl. But Daddy
was always there to help.

Daddy and Emily read books together...

...and played games, too.
Sometimes Emily let Daddy win!

On Wednesday afternoons, Emily went to ballet.

She had a pink leotard,

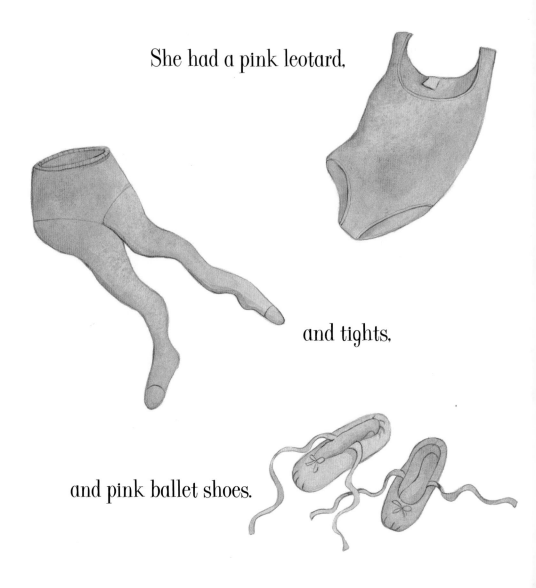

and tights,

and pink ballet shoes.

Daddy always took Emily to ballet on his bike.

He stayed to watch with the other
mommies and daddies.

"That's my little girl!" he would say
proudly, when it was Emily's turn to dance.

When Emily started school, Daddy and Emily walked
there together. Emily was too big to go on Daddy's bike.
On the way, they made up songs to sing.

When school was over, Daddy was always there
to meet Emily. Emily loved showing him what
she had done that day.
"I'm so proud of my clever little girl,"
Daddy always said.

On Emily's birthday, Mommy and Daddy gave Emily
a special present—a brand-new bike and
a matching helmet!

Emily was excited—but then she was worried.
"I don't know how to ride a bike," she said.
"Don't worry," said Daddy. "I'll teach you."

The next day, Daddy put small training wheels on Emily's new bike. Then he showed her how to get on and off the bike, and push the pedals with her feet.

Daddy stayed close by while Emily rode
up and down the sidewalk.

Before long, Emily could ride her bike really well.
One day, Daddy said, "I think it's time to take the
training wheels off!"

Emily wasn't sure, but Daddy promised he'd be
right there beside her.

Daddy held onto the back of the seat while Emily pedaled the bike.

"It feels wobbly!" Emily said.

"You're doing fine," said Daddy. "I won't let you fall."

Emily rode all the way down the street.
"I think you can let go now, Daddy," she said.

"I already have!" Daddy called. Emily was riding her bike all by herself—with no training wheels! She felt very proud.

"That's my girl!" said Daddy. He was proud, too.

Wheee!

At the weekend, Emily helped
Daddy take the special seat
off his bike.

He attached it to
Mommy's bike.

Then they all went on a bike ride in the park.

Emily's little brother rode
in the special seat...

...and Emily rode right
beside Daddy.

When they got home that evening, Daddy helped
Emily put her bike away in the garage.

"Well," he asked, "how did my little girl enjoy her
first bike ride in the park?"

"It was great, Daddy!" said Emily.

After dinner, Emily and Daddy drew some pictures.

"Daddy, will I always be your little girl?" Emily asked.

"Yes," said Daddy, smiling. "Always."

"Although I can ride a grown-up bike like yours and Mommy's?" asked Emily.

"Yes," said Daddy. "Even then. No matter how big you
get, you will always be my little girl."
Emily was glad.